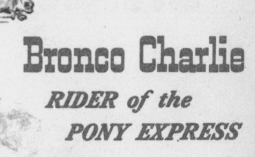

# Bronco Charlie
## RIDER of the
## PONY EXPRESS

# Bronco Charlie

# RIDER of the PONY EXPRESS

By HENRY V. LAROM

Illustrated by WESLEY DENNIS

SCHOLASTIC BOOK SERVICES

Published by Scholastic Book Services, a division
of Scholastic Magazines, Inc., New York, N. Y.

CHARLIE MILLER— the boy this story is about—was ten years old when Abraham Lincoln became President of the United States. He lived on a cattle ranch in the West. He learned to ride horses so well that the cowboys named him "Bronco Charlie."

Bronco Charlie lived to be 105 years old. He liked to tell boys and girls about his many adventures. He liked to tell about taming horses and fighting Indians. But the story of how he became a Pony Express rider is the most exciting of all.

CHARLIE MILLER lived on a big cattle ranch in California. He liked the cattle, and he liked the cowboys. But best of all he liked the horses.

All day long he sat on the fence and watched the men who gentled the wild horses and taught them to be cow ponies.

The best horse breaker of all was a Mexican. His name was John Teata, and Charlie thought he was the most wonderful rider in all the world. When John rode a wild bronco, the horse would jump and buck and spin around and around, trying to shake John off. But no matter what the bronco did, when it was all over John Teata was still on the horse's back, talking to him in soft Mexican words and patting him on the neck.

And the first thing Charlie knew, the horse was as gentle as a lamb.

Charlie was always begging John to let him ride a wild horse. But John would smile and say, "You are too young, Charlie. Some day you will be a bronco buster. But not yet. You are not old enough."

But Charlie kept right on asking.

At last John and the other cowboys decided to let him try. "You can ride this one we call the Rabbit," John said, grinning.

"Why is he called the Rabbit?" Charlie asked.

"Because he makes such big jumps," John said.

And all the cowboys laughed. They thought that at the very first jump Charlie would fall off.

They caught the wild horse called the Rabbit, and they put a blindfold on him so that he could not see Charlie.

Then they put on a saddle, and made sure it was on good and tight. Then Charlie climbed onto the Rabbit's back. He took a tight grip on the reins and tried not to look scared. The cowboys opened the gate and John pulled off the horse's blindfold.

Well, the Rabbit made the biggest jump you ever saw. He jumped up. He jumped down. He jumped all around. Then he ran away. But Charlie still stuck to his back.

All the cowboys cheered Charlie and told him to hang on. But the Rabbit slipped in a badger hole and fell down. Charlie rolled off, laughing. Then he got up, caught the Rabbit, and climbed on his back again.

But here is where Charlie got a big surprise. This time the Rabbit didn't jump. He knew he could not shake Charlie off. The Rabbit decided Charlie was the boss, and he wanted to be friends.

All the cowboys slapped Charlie on the back.

"You are a real bronco buster," John said. "And you are brave, too. From now on you help me to gentle horses, and your name will be *Bronco Charlie*. And you can have the Rabbit for your very own horse."

That was one of the happiest days in Charlie's life.

One day a man came to the ranch and bought the very best horses they had.

"What are you going to do with them?" Charlie asked.

"They are for the Pony Express," the man said.

"What is that?" Charlie's eyes were wide with interest.

"We are carrying the mail by horseback," the man said, "all the way from St. Joseph in Missouri to California. We have the fastest horses in the West, the best riders, the bravest men, and the mail comes to California faster than ever before."

Of course this was long, long ago, when the West was still wild. There were no trains that crossed the country, no cars, no airplanes, no telephones, no telegraph. Often it took months for a letter to get to California by wagon train. But the Pony Express could make it in ten days.

"How do you get to be a Pony Express rider?" Charlie asked the man.

"You have to be tough, a very good rider, and very light," the man said.

"Then I want to be a Pony Express rider," Charlie said. "I am all those things."

"You are too young," the man told Charlie.

"Going on twelve isn't young," Charlie protested.

"Yes it is," said the man. "When you're a little older, maybe you can be a rider."

Charlie dreamed every night that he was carrying the mail for the Pony Express, on a very fast horse, with very important letters, for that was the job he wanted more than anything else in the world.

Now Charlie's father was a miner, and so his mother and father lived in the mining town of Sacramento. But they thought it was better for Charlie to stay on the ranch. So Charlie could not depend on his parents for anything. He had to learn to look

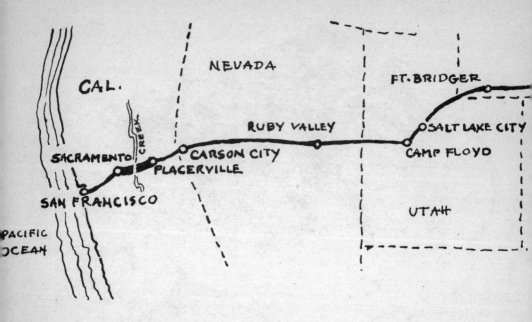

after himself when he was very young, and to be brave and face his own problems.

One day he had a chance to visit his family in Sacramento. He had never been to a town before. He thought it was very noisy, and there were too many people and not enough horses. All he wanted to see was the Pony Express station.

"All right, son," said Mr. Miller. "We will go up the street and see the Pony Express rider come in. He has to change horses, get something to eat, and gallop to Placerville."

"Then what does he do?" Charlie asked.

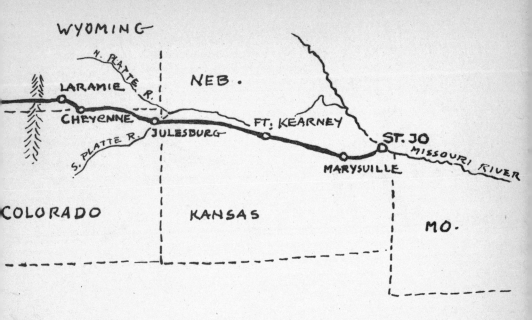

"He turns his mail pouch over to the next rider, who rides on to Carson City. Then still another rider takes it, and that goes on until finally the mail arrives at St. Jo, Missouri. It is mighty fast work. They don't waste a minute. Watch how fast he changes horses," his father said.

"But what does he do at Placerville after he turns over the mail?" Charlie asked.

"He has a good sleep," Mr. Miller said. "Then he grabs the next mail bag coming this way and brings it back here to Sacramento, and on to San Francisco."

17

"What happens when the weather gets bad in the mountains?" Charlie knew about the trails. They could be dangerous.

"Bad weather, Indians, landslides, blizzards—it doesn't matter. The Pony Express goes through."

Charlie and his father waited around the station. Then, suddenly, people began to shout. Charlie looked down the street. He saw a horse galloping toward him. It carried a saddle and a mail pouch. But the stirrups waved wildly. The saddle was empty, and there was no sign of the rider.

The agent for the Pony Express rushed out and caught the horse.

"What happened?" asked Mr. Miller.

"Don't know," the agent said, taking off the mail pouch. "Horse may have fallen with him. Or the rider might have been washed off crossing a river."

"The horse doesn't seem to be wet," Charlie broke in. "And he sure doesn't look as if he had fallen down."

19

The Pony Express man looked at Charlie sharply.

"That's right," he said. "I didn't like to say it, but it looks as though the Indians might have got him."

"What are you going to do?" Charlie asked.

"I don't know," the agent said. "This rider was supposed to go through to Placerville. There's nothing I can do until the next rider comes by. I'm afraid this time the mail won't go through."

Charlie looked up at his father and the agent. If only his father would let *him* ride and carry the mail

and be—for one day—a real Pony Express rider.

"Pa," he said. "Pa! Please tell him I can do it!"

Charlie's father looked at Charlie. He knew how Charlie felt, how brave he was. He knew Charlie could ride. He was very proud of his son for wanting to carry the mail.

The agent was standing there with a fresh horse — a beautiful dark bay, speed in every line of its body.

Charlie's father picked up Charlie and dropped

him onto the horse's back. "There's your rider," he said. "Charlie can ride anything."

The agent looked at Charlie, who was little and thin and only eleven years old. "Do you think a little boy like that can ride well enough to take the mail all the way to Placerville?" he asked. "It's over forty miles."

"I can ride anything on four legs," Charlie said. "I'll get the mail through, right on the very minute."

"He is not boasting." Mr. Miller smiled. "He can really do it."

The agent didn't like to see such a small boy with such important mail. But he had nobody else.

"All right," he said to Mr. Miller. "If you say he can do it, and you give your permission, we'll let him ride."

Charlie patted the horse's neck. It was the best-looking horse he had ever ridden, with big wise eyes, a short back, and stocky legs, good for mountain climbing.

"This horse's name is Rambler," the agent said. "He knows the trail, and he'll really ramble for you, boy!"

Then he showed Charlie the mail pouch with four pockets. Three of them were sealed in oilskin to keep out the rain. The fourth one had the orders for the other agents along the trail. The agent gave Charlie a horn. "Blow it when you get to Placerville," he said. "Then the agent there will be ready for you. And get started! You're late now."

"Good-by, Pa," Charlie said. "Good-by, mister," he said to the agent. "Don't worry. With a horse like Rambler, I could run the mail from here to China."

Then Charlie spurred Rambler into a gallop, and they disappeared over the hill.

At first, Charlie let his horse gallop as fast as he could. Then they came to the mountains. The trail grew very narrow and steep. Rambler had to scramble up and down the steep hills. Charlie let the horse's reins loose so that Rambler could keep his head down and watch the rough, rocky trail.

Charlie felt mighty proud of himself. He looked down at the wonderful horse that he was riding and at the important mail pouch tied to the saddle. At last — for one trip anyway — he knew he was a real Pony Express rider!

"I'll bet you are proud too, aren't you, Rambler?" he said to the horse.

Rambler let his ears point back, to show Charlie he was listening. And Charlie thought that maybe Rambler would become his friend.

Charlie had a pretty good idea of the trail. He recognized the mountain peak off to his left, and he knew that he must cross the shoulder of another mountain ahead of him. But just the same he was glad Rambler knew where he was going. Charlie decided that the trip was going to be fairly easy.

Then it started to rain. The rain came down so fast that the water in the creeks got higher and higher. The trail almost washed away, and it was very slippery and dangerous. Charlie got very wet indeed, and so did Rambler.

But Charlie was a cowboy. He was used to being wet. And Rambler was used to the open range all

his life. So they rode on in spite of the sheets of water. Charlie looked at the mail pouch to make sure that it was sealed tight with oiled silk and no water could get at the letters.

After a while the rain stopped, and it began to grow dark. Charlie and Rambler were deep in the mountains. And Charlie began to feel lonesome. He was used to riding at night around the cattle. But then there were cowboys for company, and they sang songs to keep the cattle quiet, and the cows and calves were company too.

But now Charlie was all alone. Even his horse was strange. And sometimes Rambler kicked a rock off the trail with his foot, and it fell into a deep canyon...bounding...bumping...crashing into the darkness below.

Charlie and Rambler kept on into the mountains, and although Charlie was a bit scared he knew the mail had to go through. A Pony Express rider never quits! He had to be brave, even when he heard a mountain lion yelping and screaming in the night.

Rambler was following a trail through the woods, and Charlie could see the moon rising through the trees. Then, suddenly, the horse stopped.

Charlie tried to see what was ahead. He wondered if the Indians were going to waylay him. They

never missed a chance to try to capture a Pony Express horse. There was a great crashing sound in the brush. Charlie was frightenend. Then he laughed. He and Rambler had scared a great big moose off the trail, and the moose was so surprised to see Charlie and Rambler that he was running away.

"I believe that big old moose was a lot more scared than we were," Charlie said. "Don't you think so, Rambler?"

Rambler flipped his ears back to show he understood, and he kept on going down a steep mountainside, watching for dangerous holes, slippery rocks, and loose gravel. Rambler knew he had to help Charlie get the mail through to Placerville.

Although Charlie didn't think there were any Indians around, he couldn't be sure. He remembered the rider who had probably run into them that very day, and he kept a sharp lookout.

A few minutes later they rounded a bend in the trail, and suddenly Charlie pulled up his horse.

Ahead of him he thought he saw an Indian against the moonlit sky. The Indian had a bow raised and an arrow ready.

Charlie held his breath and kept as quiet as he could. He waited for the Indian to move. But nothing happened. Was the Indian waiting, too?

At last Charlie could stand it no longer. He kicked Rambler and, as they jumped forward, Charlie let out a great sigh of relief. What he thought was an Indian was only an aspen tree shining in the moonlight. It only *looked* like an Indian. But just the same, Charlie was glad to ride on as fast as he could.

An hour later Charlie saw the first gray streaks of light in the east, and he knew the dawn was coming at last.

"Now we must be almost to Placerville," he said to Rambler. "And the ground is flat, so we can go faster," and he made Rambler trot over the hills.

Then, just as Charlie thought all his troubles were over, they came to a creek, and it was swollen with rain. It was too deep for Rambler to cross, and it looked very dangerous. For a while Charlie rode up

and down the bank, trying to find a place to cross. But finally he decided that there was only one thing to do. He and Rambler would have to swim.

First he made sure that the mail was well sealed. Then he pulled his feet from the stirrups and made Rambler wade into the water. "Come on, boy!" Charlie shouted over the sound of the stream. "Swim hard!" Rambler swam as hard as he could. But the current was very strong; it turned him downstream, and he had to snort to keep the water out of his nose.

Charlie was so afraid Rambler would go under that he decided to lighten the weight on the horse's back. He slid out of the saddle and hung onto the saddle horn. Rambler felt the weight leave his back. It was easier for him to swim, so he swam very hard, and finally reached the other bank and pulled Charlie out with him.

Charlie checked the mail pouch, and it was all right. He looked Rambler over, and he was all right. Then he felt over himself, where he had bumped on the rocks coming out of the creek, and he was all right too.

Charlie jumped into the saddle. "Placerville, here we come!" he shouted, and Rambler jumped into a gallop.

A few minutes later they saw Placerville below
them. It wasn't much of a town—just a few shacks
and a muddy road. But there was smoke coming

out of the chimneys. There was warmth and food for a small and very wet boy and a tired and very wet bay horse. They were both very hungry, too.

Then Charlie remembered the horn. He grabbed it up, put it to his lips, and blew it just as hard as he could.

"Get ready!" the bugle seemed to say. "Turn out, everybody! Here comes the mail! Here comes Bronco Charlie! Here comes the Pony Express!"

Charlie pulled up hard in front of the station. The agent came running out, then stopped. He certainly was surprised. "Who are you?" he asked. "What are you doing with the mail pouch?"

"I was hired on at Sacramento," Charlie said. "A relief rider."

"Well!" The agent grabbed the mail pouch. "Good for you," he said. "You're the youngest rider I've seen yet."

Another boy, older than Charlie, stood by a horse. The agent tossed the pouch to him, and he threw it across his saddle. "Get started!" the agent said.

"Shucks, I just left!" The boy winked at Charlie, leaped into the saddle, and galloped off toward Carson City, which was the next stop to the east.

When Charlie explained everything, the men at the station were very kind to him. He warmed himself by a big open fire, He filled himself with biscuits and bacon. He made sure that Rambler was getting hay and oats in the barn. Then he went to bed and fell fast asleep.

The next day Charlie took another pouch of mail
back to Sacramento. This time it was pretty easy.
It was daylight. It didn't rain. The creek was low,
and he didn't have to swim.

He galloped into Sacramento as fast as he could
go. He blew the horn. He let out a "yipee" and pulled
his horse up at the station in a big cloud of dust.

41

Then he got a big surprise. The agent ran out to get the pouch. His father ran up the street and shouted at him. His mother waved. And a whole crowd of people ran out just to see the eleven-year-old boy who carried the mail.

They gave him a big cheer. Everybody wanted to clap him on the back. His mother hugged him and kissed him. His father shook his hand. The agent thanked him and turned the mail for San Francisco over to a new rider.

And that night Charlie went to bed very happy and proud — all except for one thing... It was all over.

Tomorrow he would have to go back to the ranch. No more adventures, no more chance to carry the mail.

"If only I could be just a little older," he thought. "Then I could be a *real* Pony Express rider. I could make some money to help my father and mother. I could ride a horse as good as Rambler every day. I would have lots of adventures. I would rather be a Pony Express rider than anything else on earth."

Charlie could hear his father talking to somebody in the other room, and he couldn't go to sleep because he wanted to be a Pony Express rider. And he didn't have a chance.

But finally he did go to sleep, and the next thing he knew somebody was shaking him.

"Get up, Charlie. Get up, boy!" his father said. "I have a surprise for you."

Charlie sat up in bed. "What is it?" he asked.

"I was talking to the Pony Express agent last night," his father said. "You made such a fine ride to Placerville the other day, he wants you to be a regular rider for the Pony Express, even though you are very young."

Charlie jumped out of bed and let out a cowboy yell. He made more noise than a mountain lion.

"Will you let me, Pa?" he asked. "Will you and Ma let me?"

"Yes," Mr. Miller said. "Other boys are doing it. You are young. But you are just as brave. You are a good bronco rider, and you will be helping your country by carrying the mail. Now you get dressed." Mr. Miller poked Charlie. "We have to go up to the station. You have to be sworn in."

Well, you can imagine how happy Bronco Charlie was! But he was very solemn when he took the oath — the oath of the Pony Express rider. He had to promise to be mighty good — not to swear and not to fight or quarrel. He promised to be faithful and to be honest, and to do everything he could for the Pony Express service. Then the agent gave him a little leatherbound Bible and a big six-shooter pistol.

"You should read the Bible all the time," the agent said. "It is a very great book. But you should only use the gun for three reasons — to protect the mail, and to save your horse, and to defend yourself.

"And now, Bronco Charlie Miller, I pronounce you a real, honest-to-goodness Pony Express rider."

That was just about the finest day in Bronco Charlie's life.

Bronco Charlie had more dangerous adventures, greater excitements, and many honors in the years that followed. Yet on his one-hundredth birthday, when he looked back over his life the thing that made him proudest of all was that single memory — the day he became a rider for the Pony Express.